W9-ARU-236

NICKELODEON

Drake & Josh

Alien Invasion

NICKELODEON
Drake & Josh

Alien Invasion

Adapted by Laurie McElroy
Based on "Alien Invasion," written by Steve Holland
and "The Demonator," written by Anthony Del Broccolo
and Eric Friedman

Based on *Drake & Josh* created by Dan Schneider

SCHOLASTIC INC.
New York   Toronto   London   Auckland   Sydney
Mexico City   New Delhi   Hong Kong   Buenos Aires

If you purchased this book without a cover, you should be aware that this book is stolen property. It was reported as "unsold and destroyed" to the publisher, and neither the author nor the publisher has received payment for this "stripped book."

No part of this work may be reproduced in whole or in part, stored in a retrieval system, or transmitted in any form or by any means, electronic, mechanical, photocopying, recording, or otherwise, without written permission of the publisher. For information regarding permission, write to Scholastic Inc., Attention: Permissions Department, 557 Broadway, New York, NY 10012.

ISBN-10: 0-439-89044-6
ISBN-13: 978-0-439-89044-1

© 2007 Viacom Inc. All Rights Reserved.
Nickelodeon, Drake and Josh, and all related titles, logos, and characters are trademarks of Viacom International Inc.

Published by Scholastic Inc.

SCHOLASTIC and associated logos are trademarks and/or registered trademarks of Scholastic Inc.

12 11 10 9 8 7 6 5 4 3 2 1   7 8 9 10/0

Printed in the U.S.A.
First printing, January 2007

Alien Invasion

Part One
Alien Invasion

PROLOGUE

Drake Parker sat at the kitchen table with a huge plate of French fries in front of him. More French fries than even he could eat, so he was building a French fry fort. "All right, everyone knows that Josh can be annoying," he said.

Josh Nichols was on clean up duty in his room, doing the job he always got stuck with — putting CDs and DVDs back in their plastic cases. Drake was always leaving them lying around. "It's no secret that Drake can cause me *extreme* aggravation," he said.

"But you know who constantly drives me insane?" Drake asked. He added a couple of fries to his fort's wall.

Josh searched through the pile of empty cases, looking for the right home for the CD in his hand. "But you know who *really* gets my blood pressure up into the danger zone?"

"She's eleven," Drake said, wondering if the walls of his fort would stand up to a ketchup invasion. He decided to fortify them with a few more fries.

Josh found the right CD case and moved on to the next disc in his pile. "She's a girl." Josh said.

Drake shuddered. "She's evil."

Josh's face twisted in a sneer. "She's a demon."

"She's my little sister," Drake said with a grimace.

"Megan!" Josh said, totally exasperated by the idea that such a normal-looking girl could be so evil.

"Megan," Drake said, completed irritated by the idea that such a normal-looking girl could be so evil.

Josh had his reasons. "Last month, she put kitty litter in my sneakers," he said, remembering how awful it was to put his foot into this sneaker and discover not only the kitty litter, but evidence that the neighbor's cat had mistaken his sneakers for a litter box.

"Did you know she signed me up for the Mexican army?" Drake asked. He had spent weeks dodging a

Mexican general who insisted Drake show up for boot camp.

"And let's not forget the time she dyed all my underwear pink." Josh said, shaking his head.

"She gave my cell phone number to three hobos," Drake said, remembering another one of Megan's evil tricks.

"I do not look good in pink pants." Josh said. He'd probably be scarred for life by the teasing he got when the guys saw him changing for gym class.

"Now," Drake said with frustration. "Every time my phone rings? It's a hobo."

"But one day . . . oh. ho, ho," Josh said, nodding. "One day, baby . . ."

"One day, she's going to push me too far," Drake said with a nod.

"Revenge!" Josh shouted, waving his fist in the air. "Revenge!"

Drake's cell phone rang. He rolled his eyes and answered. "Hello?" He heard a raspy voice ask to come

over to his house. "No! Leave me alone!" Drake yelled.

Josh held a pair of pink jockey shorts next to his face. "It's just not right."

CHAPTER ONE

Josh Nichols sat at his desk working on his math homework, his textbook open in front of him. "Three times the square root of two," he said to himself.

Drake Parker came into the bedroom they shared, eating a sandwich.

Josh didn't notice. He was too focused on finding the right answer. "Minus X," he said, working on the problem with a pencil and paper. Calculators were too easy.

Drake grabbed a remote from the couch and turned on the stereo before flopping down with a music magazine. Rock and roll blared from the stereo.

Josh looked up. He was about to solve the problem, but Drake's music sent the answer right out of his head. "Hey," he yelled. Sometimes it seemed as if Drake still thought this room was all his own, that Josh didn't live there at all.

Drake flipped a page in his magazine.

"Hey," Josh yelled again, louder this time.

Drake noticed Josh for the first time. "Oh, hey," he yelled over the music. He also noticed the slightly annoyed look on Josh's face. "Want some sandwich?" Drake asked, as a peace offering. He held out his ham and cheese, but all that was left was chewed-on crust.

"No," Josh yelled back. "I'm trying to do my homework. Could you turn that off?"

Drake turned off the music and Josh went back to his homework with an annoyed shake of his head.

The bedroom they shared used to be Drake's private paradise. But when Josh's dad married Drake's mom, the guys suddenly became both brothers and roommates.

It was a super cool room, and big enough for two guys. It stretched from the front of the house to the back over the garage. It was unfinished, with exposed beams and unpainted wallboards. Drake had built a loft bed under the window, bought an old couch and comfy chairs at a yard sale, and filled the walls with posters, road signs, and old license plates.

They added a bed and a desk for Josh, and he moved in his TV and video games, too. There was nothing better than kicking back on their couch, feet up on the coffee table, listening to tunes, watching the tube, or playing video games.

But sometimes — like now — Drake forgot that he couldn't have everything his own way all the time, and Josh missed the peace and quiet of the old days, when it was just him and his dad.

Josh was just getting back to X when Drake picked up his electric guitar and started strumming a blues number.

Well my brother, Josh
He's doin' his homework

Josh glazed as Drake kept on singing. This wasn't making finding X any easier. "Would you please cut that out?" Josh asked, getting annoyed.

But Drake still wasn't done with his song.

Well ol' cranky Josh
He's gettin' so cranky
So very cranky

Josh stared straight ahead, fuming. X slipped out of his grasp again. In frustration, he snapped his pencil in half and threw the pieces into the air.

Drake kept singing, making up the song as he went along.

Oh now he's breakin' things
Writing to the pencil repairman
He'll know what to do

"Dude," Josh yelled, jumping to his feet. "Would you stop with the improvisational blues tune! Shouldn't you be doing your homework, too?"

Drake stood and pulled a folded piece of paper from his back pocket. "My homework's already taken care of," Drake answered with a cocky expression, handing the paper to Josh.

Josh opened the note and read it out loud while Drake played with a new tune on the guitar. "Please excuse Drake from doing his homework. He twisted his liver and is unable to read, write, or bathe," Josh read. "Yours truly, the doctor."

"Wrote it myself," Drake said proudly.

"Should the doctor have a name?" Josh asked.

"Ah, yes. Here, gimme that," Drake said, reaching for the note. He grabbed a pen from the coffee table and used his guitar as a writing surface. "Uh, let's see," he said, thinking. "Bob . . . the doctor," he announced, as he added the words to the note. Drake looked up with a smile. "Yeah?" he asked, handing Josh the note.

Josh looked at the note — written on wrinkled yellow notebook paper and signed by "Bob, the doctor." "Oh yeah," Josh said with a straight face, dropping the note on the coffee table. "Yeah, now it's perfect."

"Cool," Drake said with a nod. He had more important things to do than homework. He ate the final bit of his sandwich and strummed the guitar some more. He had the beginnings of an excellent new tune.

Josh looked around. Maybe it was time to give up on finding X the old fashioned way and use his computer to help him. But he didn't see it. "Hey, Drake, have you seen my laptop?" he asked.

"Yeah," Drake said, chewing. "I think Megan's using it in the backyard."

"What?" Josh yelled. "How many times do I have to tell her not to touch my stuff?" He was totally frustrated.

Whenever something important disappeared, Megan was the culprit. Josh stomped across the room. No matter how many times he told her to stay away from his stuff, Megan treated his things like they were her own personal property. "Ho, ho, I am going to fix her wagon," he said.

Drake blinked in confusion. "She doesn't have a wagon," he said.

Josh rolled his eyes. "It's a figure of speech!" he yelled, storming out of the room.

Drake went back to his blues tune.

> *Well ol' cranky Josh*
> *He's fixin' Megan's wagon*
> *But not lit-er-a-leeee*

Josh opened the door and stuck his head in. He didn't have to say anything. His expression said it for him: Stop making up songs about me!

Drake played one more chord, punctuated by the door slamming as Josh headed downstairs and into the backyard to have it out with Megan once and for all.

CHAPTER TWO

Drake didn't want to miss the fireworks so he followed his brother downstairs. They walked into the backyard to find Megan standing next to a giant telescope in the middle of the yard. Josh's laptop, on a picnic table nearby, was hooked up to the telescope so that Megan could record images from space.

"What are you doing?" Josh asked, totally annoyed.

"Studying astronomy," Megan said, equally annoyed by Josh's question.

"Ahhh," Drake said, tapping Josh on the shoulder. "The study of stars and planets." He was proud of himself — there was actually something he could explain to Josh.

"Yes," Josh mocked. "It's exciting to know things." Then he turned back to Megan. "Now give me my laptop back." He walked over to the table to collect his property.

"No!" Megan ran over and stopped him. "I need it."

"For what?" Josh asked.

"Mom just bought me this really cool telescope that you can hook up to a computer. Here check this out," she said, shoving Josh out of her way. She typed on the keyboard as she explained. "I just type in the name of the any planet or constellation I want to see, and then the computer tells the telescope where to point." Megan was so into her new telescope that she forgot how annoying her brothers could be. She was having fun showing them how the telescope worked.

"Look," Megan said, hitting the enter key.

Drake and Josh stepped in closer. The telescope made a humming sound as it moved, zeroing in on its new target.

"And you can see the image right on the screen!" Megan said, her voice rising with excitement. "How cool is that?"

And there it was, a giant close up of the moon on the laptop's screen.

But Josh wasn't going to be swayed by astronomy images — no matter how cool they were. "Why can't you use your own laptop?" he asked.

"Because!" Megan insisted. "I'm not bringing my laptop outside. It could get wet or something."

"She's got a point," Drake said, leaning in to get a closer look at the moon.

"She's got no point!" Josh claimed. Why should his laptop be the one to risk getting wet?

"Oh, calm down," Drake said. "So she's using your laptop. What's the big deal?" Josh didn't know it, but Drake used his brother's laptop all the time.

"Thank you," Megan said to Drake, moving back to her telescope.

Drake watched her go, and then noticed that her telescope was resting on top of something — something leather. "Hey . . . hey!" he yelled, pointing at the ground. "What's that under your telescope?"

Megan widened her eyes innocently. "What?" she asked, pretending not to understand.

"Is that my new leather jacket?" Drake asked with his hands on his hips.

"Maybe," Megan said with a shrug.

"Megan!" Drake shouted in complete exasperation. It had him taken three months worth of band gigs to save enough money to buy that jacket. And now it was laying on the grass with a telescope on top of it!

"Well, I'm not putting my brand new telescope on the grass," she said, crossing her arms over her chest.

"She's got a point," Josh said, mocking.

Drake only had his brother's words to fall back on. "She's got no point!" he insisted. "I want my jacket back!"

"Yeah, and I want my laptop!" Josh added.

"*Okaaaay*, fine," Megan said, sounding resigned. "Just one sec." Then she walked around the front of the telescope and looked for a comfortable spot before lying down on her back in the grass.

Drake and Josh were both confused.

"What are you doing?" Josh asked.

Megan didn't answer.

"Hey, what's she doing?" Drake asked his brother.

Megan crossed her ankles and rested her hands on her stomach. Then, suddenly, she let out a loud, high-pitched scream. The neighbor's dog started to bark.

Drake and Josh stood over her, more confused than ever.

"What's going on?" Josh asked.

Drawn by Megan's scream, Walter Nichols dashed out of the house. "What happened?" he asked.

Megan sat up and pretended to be on the verge of tears. "Well I was just out here trying to learn about space, and Drake and Josh pushed me down."

Walter's eyes widened in disbelief. He turned to the guys. "What?" he asked, outraged.

Drake and Josh looked at each other, then at Mr. Nichols.

"We didn't push her down!" Drake said.

"Oh, right," Megan said sarcastically. She got to her feet and brushed the grass off her jeans. "I just decided to lie down on the grass and scream."

"Yes," Josh said, pointing at her. "That's exactly what you did."

An angry Walter cut him off. "Boys! Stop taunting your little sister and go upstairs."

Josh tried to defend himself against Megan's false accusations. "Dad, we didn't do anything."

Drake's words tumbled over his brother's. "But we didn't."

Mr. Nichols cut them both off with his angry expression. "Go upstairs," he ordered through clenched teeth.

Drake and Josh both glared at Megan as they headed into the house.

Mr. Nichols drew Megan into a comforting hug and patted her on the back. He didn't notice the evil smile playing on her lips.

Seconds later, Drake slammed into his bedroom, followed by Josh.

"Can you believe her?" Drake fumed.

"She aggravates me in so many ways," Josh agreed. He furiously paced across the floor. "Ho, ho, I am whipped up, man!"

"We have got to do something about her!" Drake said. He grabbed a couple of sodas from their mini fridge and tossed a can to Josh.

Josh rolled his eyes. They had tried this before, and Megan always managed to get the better of them in the end. That little girl lived to torture her brothers, and she excelled at it. If teachers gave grades for being super-annoying, Megan would be at the head of her class. "Yeah, like what?" Josh asked, climbing up to sit on the edge of Drake's loft bed.

Drake thought for a minute. The icy-cold soda gave him an idea. "Okay, I've got it! We freeze her," he said, his eyes lighting up. "Yeah! Then, we thaw her out like three hundred years into the future." Drake imagined Megan waking up in the future world. He would be standing over her with his arms crossed over his chest and a big grin on his face. That would be so cool! "Oh man, she will be so freaked out," he said.

"Okay," Josh said slowly, pretending Drake's idea was one they could actually follow through with. "Let me write that down." He grabbed a pad and pen and pretended to write. "Freeze her."

Drake realized he was being mocked. "You didn't really write it down."

"No!" Josh yelled, throwing the pad and pen up into the air. Megan had made him lose all patience with Drake's screwball ideas.

"Well, fine. You got something better?" Drake challenged.

Josh jumped off the loft bed and started pacing again, thinking. He came to a dead stop when an idea came to him — an excellent idea. "Yeah. Okay, Megan's really into her telescope, right?"

"Yeah," Drake answered.

"Well, what if she saw something in her telescope that totally freaked her out?" Josh asked with a grin.

Drake grinned too, and thought about the moon image they had just seen. "Dad's butt?" he asked.

Josh lowered his voice to a whisper. "Freakier."

"Wow," Drake said, whispering too.

"Yeah," Josh answered. His head was spinning with all the details. This was going to be amazing. And Megan was finally going to get a little of what was coming to her.

CHAPTER THREE

A little while later, Megan was still using her telescope to study the night sky. She stepped on Drake's leather jacket on her way over to Josh's laptop, and typed a few words on the keyboard. The telescope pivoted, and she looked through the eyepiece at one of Saturn's rings and then back at the computer screen. This was so cool!

Drake and Josh peered out from behind a bush when they heard the back door open and close.

Their mother, Audrey Nichols, came outside. "Hey, sweetie," she said to Megan. "Listen, take a break and go help your dad with the dishes."

Megan turned to her mother and made a face. "Aw, but what if he talks to me?" she asked. Megan loved her stepfather, but he was always expecting her to laugh at his dorky jokes.

"Hey, I put up with it," Mrs. Nichols joked, leading Megan into the house. "You can, too."

The brothers popped up from behind the bushes.

Drake just walked up to the laptop, but Josh acted like he was a secret agent in a spy movie. He climbed over a garden bench and dropped to a crouch in the grass. Then he suddenly pivoted in the other direction to see if he was being watched before calling Drake forward with a fake birdcall.

Drake rolled his eyes at Josh's silly stealth fighter routine, but there was nothing silly about Josh's computer know how. Drake was just there to assist.

"Give me the DVD," Josh said, holding out his hand like a surgeon. He had already typed in some commands and opened the laptop's DVD drive.

Drake pulled the disc out of the waistband of his jeans and put it into Josh's hand.

"Eeewww," Josh said, grimacing. "You put my copy of *Alien Attack Two* down your pants?"

"So?" Drake asked.

Josh was totally grossed out. "It's all warm," he said.

"Just hurry," Drake said. They didn't have time for Josh to get all freaked out over a warm DVD. Megan was the one who was supposed to get freaked, not Josh.

"All right." Josh opened the case and put the

disc into the DVD drive. "Now, when the DVD loads, I'll take a still frame of the space shuttle using Photo Doc."

Drake leaned in close.

"Then, with the cropping tool, I'll be . . ." Josh stopped. He had a pained look on his face. "Please don't breathe in my ear," he said.

"Oh, sorry." Drake stepped away slightly.

Josh got back to work.

Meanwhile, Megan helped Mr. Nichols with the dishes.

"You know, some people hate doing the dishes. But I think it's kind of fun." Mr. Nichols washed while Megan dried. He happily scrubbed away, wearing rubber gloves to protect his hands. "Don't you think it's kind of fun?" he asked.

"Yes," Megan said, with a robot-like expression. "This is kind of fun."

"So, what's your favorite part?" Mr. Nichols asked. "The scrubbing, the drying, or the stacking?"

"Wow, they're all just so much fun it's hard to pick," Megan answered, trying not to roll her eyes.

Mr. Nichols didn't know she was just humoring him. "I know! Hey, aren't we having too much fun together?" he said with a laugh, bumping her with his hip.

Megan forced herself to laugh, too, but it wasn't very convincing. "Oh, Walter," she said with a forced smile.

Josh was still trying to work his magic on his laptop.

Drake looked over his shoulder to make sure Megan wasn't on her way out. It seemed like Josh was taking an awfully long time. What if they got caught? Dad was already mad at them. "Are you sure this is gonna work?" he asked.

"Yeah," Josh answered, totally immersed in his task. He pointed to the laptop's screen. Two windows were open, side by side. One was the image of Earth's moon from Megan's telescope. The other had a picture of the spaceship from *Alien Attack Two*. "See? I just cut around the image of the spaceship from the movie."

Drake watched Josh cut around the spaceship picture on screen.

"Then I drag the picture of the spaceship into the window with Megan's telescope image," Josh explained.

Drake watched his brother paste the image of the spaceship right in front of the moon. It looked like it was flying past, on its way to Earth.

"And bam!" Josh said. "We've got aliens."

But there was no time for Drake to admire Josh's work. They heard Megan on her way back out to the yard.

"Wait," they heard Mr. Nichols say. "Do you want to help me vacuum?"

"No thanks, Walter," Megan answered.

"Megan's coming," Drake hissed. "C'mon! Hide."

Josh scrambled to eject the DVD from the computer.

"Hurry," Drake urged. He tried to hide behind a chair, but there wasn't enough coverage.

Josh jackknifed and tried to hide his head like an ostrich, then realized his butt was sticking up in the air. Megan was sure to notice that.

Then Drake spotted the garbage cans in the back of the yard. "C'mon, the cans!" he said as he jumped into one.

"All right. Good idea, dude," Josh said, trying to dive in after him. But there wasn't room for two. Josh's legs were kicking in the air.

There was no way Drake could lower the lid with Josh in there with him. "What are you doing? There's a can right there!" Drake said, pointing to the one next to his.

"I don't want to get in there alone," Josh whined. He didn't want to say it out loud, but it was dark in there. It was exactly the kind of place spiders would like.

"Oh, just get in the can!" Drake yelled, pushing Josh out of his hiding spot and lowering the lid on his can.

Josh jumped into the other trash can just in time. He closed the lid as Megan opened the back door and crossed the yard.

"Okay, now let's see what's going on up in the sky," she said to herself. She checked out the computer screen. "Okay, let's see what —"

Drake and Josh peeked out from their hiding places just in time to see Megan's jaw drop. She did a double take. Could that actually be what she thought it was? She leaned in for a closer look. It was.

"No way! A spaceship?" she said to herself. "It is a spaceship!" she yelled excitedly. "Mom! Dad! I see a spaceship!" Megan ran into the house screaming. "I see a spaceship!"

As soon as Megan was inside, the brothers lifted the lids of their trash cans and poked their heads out.

They could still hear Megan yelling. "Mom! Dad! A spaceship!"

Josh cracked up. "Did you hear that? She totally bought it!"

Together the brothers imitated Megan's excited cheer. "I see a spaceship! I see a spaceship!"

"Oh, man," Drake said. "We finally got Megan."

The guys knuckle touched and laughed some more. They had been trying to get back at Megan for a long, long time. And they had finally done it. Life was sweet — very, very sweet!

They could still hear Megan talking inside. "Dad I swear, I saw an alien ship!"

Walter Nichols's response was exactly what they expected. He was being nice, but he obviously didn't believe Megan. Who would? "Yeah, sure you did," he said.

Josh was about to climb out of his can, but Drake noticed that Dad's voice was getting louder.

"Ooo! Dad's coming," Drake said. "Back inside!"

The guys ducked back down and pulled the trash cans' lids closed just in time.

Walter made his way across the backyard with the kitchen's garbage in his hands, talking to himself as he walked. "Spaceship," he muttered to himself, shaking his head. "She sees spaceships."

He was too preoccupied to look at the computer screen. Mr. Nichols held the small kitchen garbage can as far away from his nose as he could, but a foul odor was rising from it. Yesterday's fish, maybe? Or a rotten piece of fruit? Whatever it was, the stench was totally disgusting. He opened one of the trash cans and kept his head turned way from it while he dumped the garbage. He made his way back into the house, still muttering about spaceships.

Drake stood as soon as he heard the back door close. His time in the garbage can had been a little dark and smelly, but he was still clean.

Josh's experience was a little different. He stood slowly, looking shell-shocked. A black-and-yellow banana peel was stuck to his lower lip. Lettuce and paper towels trailed down from his head like a stocking cap. And something that smelled really, really bad was sitting at his neck, ready to slip down his shirt collar. He shook himself like a dog after a rainstorm to jiggle all the garbage loose. Yuck!

CHAPTER FOUR

The next night, Drake and Josh came home to find Megan sitting at the table in the living room with a lot of expensive-looking shortwave radio equipment in front of her. Squeaks and squawks came out of the speakers as Megan fiddled with some knobs.

The guys looked at each other and grinned.

"So, whatcha doing there?" Drake asked

"Well, if I tell you something you promise to keep it a secret," Megan said, eyeing her brothers with a serious expression.

"Sure," Drake said.

"Absolutely," Josh added.

"Okay," Megan said slowly. "Last night I saw . . ." she stopped to look over her shoulder and make sure no one else was listening. "I saw a U.F.O.," she said dramatically.

Josh pretended to be shocked, but he was a super bad actor. "No way!" he said, gasping.

"Really?" Drake asked, pretending to be interested. His acting was no better than Josh's.

Megan seemed not to notice. "Swear," she said. "It was an alien spaceship, no doubt about it." Her definite tone of voice made it clear — Megan was sure about what she saw.

"Well, that's incredible," Drake said, looking at Josh.

"Astonishing," Josh agreed.

Megan fiddled with the knobs again, trying to get a clear sound. She didn't see her brothers exchange satisfied grins.

"So, what's up with the crazy radio?" Josh asked.

"I'm trying to see if I can pick up any alien transmissions," Megan said, turning some more knobs. "If they're close enough that I can see them, I should be able to hear them, too."

"Okay," Josh said, pretending to go along.

"You be careful now," Drake added, patting Megan on the head.

The guys had to bite back their laughter in the living room. They didn't want to crack up right in front of Megan and give themselves away. But as soon as the kitchen door closed behind them they burst out laughing.

"Oh man, this is awesome!" Drake said.

"Priceless! She totally believes she saw a real space-ship!" Josh said. He held his stomach. It hurt from laughing so hard.

"Oh, yeah," Drake said, catching his breath. "This so beats any prank she ever pulled on us."

"Oh, yeah!" Josh agreed.

They watched Megan through the pass-through window into the living room. She had an intense expression on her face while she twisted and turned knobs, searching for alien conversations.

"Man, just look at her," Drake said. "Sitting there trying to pick up *alien transmissions*."

Josh laughed some more, but then watching Megan listen to the shortwave radio gave him another idea. "Hey, what do you say we help her along?"

"Help her out how?" Drake asked, intrigued.

"Craig and Eric are in the ham radio club at school," Josh said. "We could borrow a transmitter and have some fun."

Drake rubbed his hands together. "Oh we could,

and we should," he said with a grin. This prank was getting better and better.

"C'mon," Josh said, heading upstairs to call his friends.

"Okay," Drake said, but there was still something he was confused about. "Hey, why would they name a radio after ham?"

"I don't know," Josh said.

"I like ham," Drake added.

"Who doesn't?"

The next night, Drake snuck into their neighbor's backyard and peered at Megan from behind a fence. She sat at the picnic table with Josh's laptop, her high-tech radio, and the telescope. She moved from one to the other, turning knobs, typing on the keyboard, and adjusting the eyepiece.

Megan looked up at the stars in the sky and wondered which one of those blinking white lights was really a spaceship. "C'mon aliens," she said, adjusting the radio frequency. "Where are you?"

Drake sunk back behind the fence and stifled a laugh. This was getting better and better. He crept through the neighbor's yard and to his own front door, racing upstairs to share the news with Josh.

"Hey!" he said, coming into the bedroom.

Josh sat in front of a ham radio with a big antenna. "Hey! Is she out there?" he asked.

"Yep," Drake snorted. "She keeps looking up at the sky wondering where the aliens are."

Josh laughed. "Perfect!" He waved his brother over. "All right. C'mere!" Josh pointed to the electronic equipment in front of him. "This is the ham radio."

Drake nodded. "Ham radio."

"We just talk into this mic," Josh said, picking up a microphone, "and sound like aliens."

Drake's face lit up. He had lots of experience talking and singing into microphones with his band. This was going to be easy. "Oh, cool. Gimme it." He took the microphone, pressed the on button, and started to talk in a deep voice. "Bonjour, s'il vous plait."

In the backyard, Megan's forehead wrinkled in confusion. She had set the radio frequencies to pick up outer space, not France. Why could she hear someone saying *hello* and *please* in French.

Inside, Drake tried to laugh with a French accent, and then babbled some more French words. "Haw, haw, haw. Oui, oui. Merci."

Josh grabbed the microphone. "We're supposed to sound like we're from outer space," he said, his voice rising in anger. "Not Paris!"

Drake looked at his brother's frustrated expression. Wasn't Josh taking himself a little too seriously? And how was Drake supposed to speak alien? He was human. "You know, there's a way to correct people nicely," he said.

Josh ignored him. He held the mic up to his mouth and turned it on. "Zeeeeeef," he said, in a high-pitched voice.

Drake chuckled and imitated him. "Zeef."

Josh held his hand over the mic. "C'mon," he said. "Do it with me."

Drake leaned in and they talked into the mic together.

"Gerkmulr. Sheezfoo," Drake said, in a high-pitched, nasally voice like Josh's.

Megan's eyes widened. Was that what she thought

it was? She sat up straight and started turning the radio's knobs, trying to make the sound clearer. "Oh. My. Gosh," she said.

More alien words came through the radio. "Gweeeeeeg," said a voice.

Megan's jaw dropped. "Gweeeeg," she shouted. "He said gweeeeg!"

Drake and Josh were starting to have fun. Their words tumbled over each other.

"Dah-zog sorna glog. Oh cheem leezpa joon-joon bleef paga-paga neeep!" Drake imagined he was saying, "Gotcha, you evil little sister," in Martian.

Josh made his alien voice even more nasally. "Na-wa-wa soordo xeet zooa. Herrro dota maga-sasa belet sorg." That was his way of saying "You will never mock Josh again," in Saturnese.

Megan was typing furiously on the laptop's keyboard, trying to capture the alien transmission. "Wow! Wow!" she shouted. "Oh, wow!"

Drake and Josh couldn't hear her. They kept babbling away in alien.

Megan was totally amazed. She stood up and yelled, "Aliens! I heard aliens!" She ran into the house.

"Aliens! I heard aliens!" Her mom and dad weren't downstairs. Megan ran to the second floor shouting. "I just heard aliens on my radio! Aliens on my radio!"

The guys heard the back door slam and then Megan's voice getting louder. They quickly stopped talking into the microphone and threw a blanket over their radio. They tried to look casual when their door flew open. Drake put his feet up on the coffee table. Josh grabbed a harmonica and leaned back on the couch, pretending to play.

"I heard aliens!" Megan yelled, totally out of breath. "Aliens." She ran out of the room, slamming the door behind her, to go in search of her parents. "Alieeeeennnnssss," she shouted as she made her way down the hall and back downstairs.

Drake and Josh cracked up. Tears streamed down their faces from laughing so hard. Megan had totally fallen for their prank.

Josh was ready to let Megan her know that they had finally gotten the better of her. "Shall we go downstairs and tell her this whole alien thing was a big joke?" Josh asked.

But Megan hadn't reached her maximum

embarrassment point yet. Drake knew revenge would be sweeter after a few more days. "Oh, no-no-no-no-no," he said with an evil laugh. "This whole alien thing has just begun."

Josh laughed along with him. He could see that Drake was already plotting their next move.

CHAPTER FIVE

The next day after school Drake watched impatiently while Eric worked on the kitchen's light switch. Eric was one of Josh's old friends from the chess club. He was a classic nerd, exactly the kind of guy Josh had been before Drake's coolness started to rub off on him. Eric had a bad haircut and thick glasses. He dressed in a classic dork wardrobe, complete with argyle sweater vests. Today's was yellow.

"How's it coming?" Drake asked for the tenth time in ten minutes.

"Don't pressure me!" Eric said. "I'll get pimples."

Drake stepped back, his arms up in mock surrender.

Just then, Josh walked in the back door. "Hey," he said.

"Hey! What time does Megan get home from oboe practice?" Drake asked.

Josh checked his watch. "A few minutes. Why?"

"Cause I had Craig hook up all the electrical stuff in the kitchen to a remote control." He was so excited about sharing his plan with Josh that he didn't notice his "friend" glare at him when he called him by the wrong name.

"For what?" Josh asked, reaching into the refrigerator for a bottle of water.

"You see, she was watching this show last night about aliens. It said that if they ever got close to Earth, their spacecrafts would mess up all kinds of electrical fields," Drake explained.

Eric finished screwing the light switch back in place. "Okay, I'm done," he said. "Here's the remote."

"Awesome," Drake said, taking it from him. The nerd had done his job, now it was time for him to go away. He looked over his shoulder, surprised to see that the guy was still standing there. "You should probably be getting home, huh?"

Figures, Eric thought. The minute he was finished doing a job for Drake, he was expected to leave. Drake never wanted to just hang out, and half the time when he saw Eric coming in the halls at school, he turned the other way. "You know," Eric said. "Sometimes I feel you just use me."

Drake shook his head. That was true, but there was no way he was going to admit it. "Oh, c'mon, Craig," Drake said, patting him on the shoulder. "You're my friend."

"I'm Eric," Eric said flatly.

Josh cut them off. "Megan just got dropped off," he said, looking out the window.

"Awesome." Drake slipped the remote control into his pocket. "Well, you know the way out," he said to Eric.

Eric pursed his lips and nodded, heading for the back door.

Drake turned to his brother. "Okay, when Megan comes in, follow my lead."

Josh nodded and leaned against the counter nonchalantly. He heard the front door slam.

"Hello," Megan called out.

Drake raised his voice so Megan would hear him. "I don't know, Josh," he said, innocently. "Maybe we should call an electrician."

Megan came into the kitchen carrying her oboe case. "Call an electrician for what?" she asked.

"Well, it's weird, but all day long . . ." Drake pressed a button on the remote and the blender suddenly turned on all by itself.

"Whoa! What is up with the blender?" Josh asked. His acting hadn't gotten any better since the other day.

Drake was stiff and awkward, too. "I don't know," he answered. He still had his hand in his pocket and pressed another button. "There goes the garbage disposal," he said, as it started to whir and grind.

Josh peered into the sink. "Well that is downright odd," he said.

Megan looked around the kitchen, her eyes wide with fear. Next the lights started flickering. The microwave and the radio turned on and off, on and off.

"Yeah," Drake said. "What's with all the electrical problems?"

"It's the aliens!" Megan announced, sounding scared.

"What?" Josh asked.

"Nooooo," said Drake, trying to soothe her.

"Yes!" Megan insisted. "Their spacecrafts make electrical stuff act all crazy!"

Josh chuckled and shook his head. "Megs," he said,

like she was the cutest thing in the world. "There's no such thing as aliens."

But Megan was in full panic mode as the lights continued to flicker and kitchen appliances turned off and on all by themselves. "There are too! I saw them and I heard them and now they're coming!" She ran out of the kitchen screaming. "Alieeeeennnnssss!"

Her brothers cracked up. Josh imitated her high-pitched scream as Megan ran through the house. "Alieeeeennnnssss!"

That night, Walter and Audrey Nichols were dressed up for an evening out. Megan sat on the couch in the living room trying to convince them to stay home with her. "Do you guys have to go play cards tonight?" she asked. "I don't want to stay home by myself."

"What about Drake and Josh?" Mr. Nichols asked.

"Sorry," Josh said, reaching for his jacket.

"Yeah, we're going to a concert," Drake said, waving two tickets in the air.

Asking didn't work. Now Megan tried whining. "Mommmmmmmm . . ." She said, stretching the word out to two syllables.

Audrey Nichols sat down on the couch and put her arm around Megan. "Oh, baby, you'll be fine," she said, rubbing her back. "You've stayed by yourself lots of times before."

"Yeah, and you babysit for that little boy across the street," Walter Nichols added.

But Megan wasn't comforted. "Yes," she snapped. "He's not an alien who's going to eat my face."

"Megan," Josh said innocently "There's no such thing as aliens."

"Yeah," Mr. Nichols agreed. "And if there were, they wouldn't just eat your face. They'd eat all of you."

Mrs. Nichols glared at her husband. Did he seriously think he was helping here?

"Well, why would they stop at the face?" Walter asked, defensively.

Mrs. Nichols rolled her eyes. "Can we just go," she said, putting an end to the alien discussion and kissing Megan on the forehead.

Mr. Nichols leaned in. "You're going to be fine," he said. "We'll see you later, okay?" He followed his wife to the door. "Have a good time, guys. Bye."

"Have a good time," Josh said.

"See you guys," Drake added.

But Megan silently fumed. She couldn't believe they were actually leaving her home alone with aliens on the loose.

Drake watched his parents leave, and then turned to Megan. "Well, we're going to that concert," he said.

"Later, Megs." Josh said with a smile.

"Fine," Megan said, jumping to her feet and storming across the room. "But when the aliens have me as an hors d'oeuvre, you'll feel really bad." She marched upstairs, her angry feet pounding the steps as she went.

"Wow," Josh said, wondering if they should call the whole thing off. "Megan's really scared and upset."

Drake didn't share his brother's concern. "Yeah, I know," he grinned. "High five!"

Josh grinned back and gave his brother a high five. The next step in their plan had driven any remaining guilt right out of his mind.

CHAPTER SIX

Minutes later, Drake climbed in his bedroom window. He and Josh had made Megan think they were going to a concert, but they had crept around the side of the house and climbed a ladder into their room. It was time to put their newest plan into action.

Drake tried to help Josh in, but Josh was stuck. "C'mon," Drake said.

"I'm coming," Josh answered, frustrated. His foot was stuck on something under the window ledge.

Drake gave a big pull and Josh's foot came loose. Josh practically flew through the window and flopped on the floor with a loud bang. It was a good thing Megan was too scared of aliens to come and investigate a noise, Drake thought.

Josh wobbled to his feet and went back to the window. "Okay, I'm in," he said, sticking his head out. "Denise, c'mon! Hurry!"

"Don't rush me," said a voice. "I'm coming."

"You're sure this lady can make us look like real aliens, right?" Drake asked his brother.

"Oh yeah, totally," Josh answered. "She did all the special effects makeup for *Ghostmonsters*."

"Where'd you find her?" Drake asked.

"She's Mindy's third cousin," Josh answered proudly. Mindy was Josh's girlfriend. He still couldn't believe that he actually had a girlfriend, let alone one with cool cousins.

"Well, she better be good for what we're paying her," Drake said.

Denise made it to the top of the ladder and stuck her head in the window just in time to hear Drake's last statement. "You're not paying me enough to be climbing up the side of your house and in through your window," she snapped, handing her makeup case to Josh. "I think a spider crawled down my neck!"

Drake and Josh tried to help her through the window, but they pulled a little too hard. Denise flopped to the floor with nearly as loud a bang as Josh did. The brothers tried to help her up.

"Don't touch! Don't touch my person!" she said, slapping their hands away.

"Are you okay?" Josh asked.

"Yes. All that climbing made me sweaty." She couldn't wait to do her job and get home. "I need a bubble bath," she announced, fanning herself with her hand.

Josh didn't want to hear all these complaints. He wanted to pull their final prank on Megan and see her face when they yelled *Gotcha!* "Look, just turn us into aliens and you can take a bath later."

"Okay, pushy," Denise answered. "Let me see your faces." She put her hands on Drake's skin and examined his features. "Your skin is flawless," she said. "Leave it to Mindy to find herself a fine boyfriend like you."

Drake grimaced and moved away. He wasn't a huge fan of Josh's girlfriend. In fact, he hated her. Mindy was the last girl he would date.

Josh stepped up. "Actually," he said with a big smile. "I'm Mindy's boyfriend." He changed his expression a few times, to show Denise his flawless skin and pearly whites.

Denise's face fell. "Oh," was all she could say. Denise took Josh's face into her hands and eyed him like the professional she was. "Yeah, you need work," she said flatly.

It was a foggy night. Megan was in the backyard. If aliens were coming, she wanted to be prepared. She fine-tuned her radio frequencies, checked her telescope, and then looked up into the sky, waiting.

Suddenly she heard a loud noise, like an engine. Colored lights started to swirl and flash in the sky. The lights and the noise came closer and closer.

Megan stood up slowly. "Hello? Hello?" she called, sounding frightened. "Who's out there? Hello?"

She heard voices coming from behind the fence. "Dah-zog sorna glog." It sounded just like the alien transmission she had heard the other night.

"Who said that?" Megan yelled in a scared voice.

The back gate flew open and two aliens lurched into the yard with threatening expressions. Megan's eyes widened in absolute terror. She backed away. They kept coming toward her.

The aliens had green hands and faces. Their skin

was covered in wrinkles and warts. They each had two creepy horns growing out of their heads, and slimy-looking worm-like things instead of hair. They wore red space suits and had big, black shields behind their heads.

They closed in on her, muttering in their alien language. Their voices were deep and raspy.

"Cheem leezpa joon joon bleef paga-paga neeeep!" said one.

"Bleef tweegbor noop fwaza. Safa-gwomka hoodle peez vooon swog," said the other.

"Leave me alone," Megan said, sounding totally terrified. "You better not eat my face! Stay away!" Megan backed into the step leading in the house and fell on her back, screaming.

The aliens kept coming. They were practically on top of her. Megan could feel their hot alien breath on her face.

"What are you doing?" she asked, trying to scoot away from them on her back.

"One," said one of the aliens.

"Two," said the other.

"Three . . ."

Megan was trapped. She held up her hands to shield herself. "What are you going to do?"

The aliens stopped and looked at each other. "Dance," they said in unison, using their regular voices.

Drake and Josh launched into a happy dance, celebrating their victory over Megan. They waved their arms, shook their hips, and stamped their feet. Then together they stopped and yelled, "Gotcha!"

Megan's face crumpled in confusion. "What?" she asked.

The aliens pulled off their masks to reveal that they were Drake and Josh. They cracked up when they saw Megan's jaw drop.

Megan stared at them open-mouthed. She was totally shocked. "Drake? Josh?"

"Ho, ho, that's right, little girl," Josh said, completely enjoying this moment. "Finally after all these years, we got you good!"

"Yeah," Drake said smugly. "How does it feel to be on the other end of a prank? Huh?"

Megan got to her feet, her eyes flashing. "Okay, that was the meanest thing ever," she said.

"Good!" Josh answered. "Maybe it'll teach you a little lesson."

"Yeah, I bet next time you'll think twice before you try one of your little —" But Drake was suddenly cut off by weird voices coming from Megan's radio. They sounded just like aliens. "What was that?" he asked Josh.

Josh was just as confused. "I don't know," he said.

"All right, c'mon," Megan said. "Joke's over. Just stop it." She ran over to the laptop to try and find out what was happening.

"It isn't us!" Josh insisted.

All of a sudden, bright-colored lights flashed in the sky. There was a hum in the air and it got louder and louder.

"I'm serious," Megan shouted, typing on the keyboard. "This isn't funny anymore."

Now Josh was getting scared. Whatever was making that loud humming noise was coming closer. "Drake, what's going on?"

"I don't know," Drake said, his voice filled with tension.

The lights got brighter, and then the yard was filled with colorful fog and a whooshing noise.

"What was that?" Megan asked, on the verge of tears.

A huge alien stepped out of the fog. He looked to Josh like he was about ten-feet-tall, with red eyes and huge snaking tentacles growing out of his head. He had sharp claws instead of fingers. The creature growled at them.

Josh tried to back away but he was frozen in his spot, too terrified to move. His eyes almost bugged out of his head and his face twisted in terror. "It's a real alien," he screamed in a high-pitched voice.

Megan screamed as loudly as she could.

"Run!" Drake shouted.

Drake's order helped Josh snap out of his shocked state and the brothers took off. They ran right into the fence, and then tried to climb over it, looking over their shoulders as the alien moved toward them with his arms wide open. He looked like he wanted to snatch them up and take them back to his home planet.

"What the?" Drake said, but he couldn't finish

the question. An image of creepy alien scientists experimenting on his human body flashed through Drake's mind. He noticed the open gate and ran through it.

Josh made one last attempt to make it over the fence before he collapsed on the ground. The alien was still coming at him. Finally, Josh took one big leap into the fence and knocked it down. Megan was still yelling in the background when he took off after Drake, screaming like a little girl. The last thing he saw was the alien lumbering awkwardly up to Megan. Josh wondered if he should try to help, but then decided that when it came to alien invasions, it was every man for himself.

Megan screamed once more, and then broken into a big smile. "Nice job, Danny."

The alien dropped his arms. "Sure thing, Megan," said the alien.

Megan peered around the fence. Drake and Josh were running so fast that she couldn't even see them, despite their bright red alien space suit costumes.

"Those dolts won't stop running till they hit Mexico," she said with a happy smirk.

Danny chuckled and put his arm around her. "Hey, can you make me some coffee?" he asked.

"Sure," Megan said, leading him into the house.

A few minutes later, she had a freshly brewed pot. "Coffee's ready," she said through the kitchen's pass-through window.

Danny was relaxing on the couch, watching TV, still wearing his alien costume. "Awesome," he said.

"How do you take it?" Megan asked.

"Black's fine."

"Cool," Megan said, pouring a cup.

Just then, the front door opened and Walter and Audrey Nichols walked in. They had come home early, a little worried about Megan. They hoped she hadn't spent the whole night sitting on the couch scared to death.

"Hi," Mrs. Nichols said.

"We're home," Mr. Nichols called.

Mrs. Nichols didn't hear a response. "Megan?"

"In the kitchen," Megan said.

"Hey sweetie," Mrs. Nichols said, coming into the kitchen and seeing Megan with the pot of coffee in her hand. "You're making coffee?"

"Not for me," Megan explained. "For a friend."

"What friend?" Mrs. Nichols asked.

Walter walked into the living room and dropped his keys on the table. Suddenly he saw a huge alien, using his claws to change channels on the remote control. He stopped and did a double take just as the alien turned to him.

"What's up?" Danny asked.

Walter's eyes got wide. His mouth dropped open. He screamed like a little girl, ran across the living room, and jumped out of the window — right through the glass.

Danny shrugged.

Megan did her best not to crack up. She'd have to find some way to blame Drake and Josh or the cost of that window would come out of her allowance.

Her brothers were probably still running, she thought. Had they seriously believed they could pull a practical joke on her? Hah! Like that was ever going to happen. Didn't they know that this was what she was best at?

Megan was still the queen of pranks in this family — now and forever.

Part Two
The Demonator

PROLOGUE

Josh hung out in his room, playing with an old yo-yo he found in a desk drawer. "My brother Drake?" he said, winding the string. "He's all about immediate gratification."

Drake Parker was in the kitchen, pacing nervously in front of the oven. "There're brownies in there," he said, peering through the oven's window. "And I want them."

"Immediate gratification means when you want

something, you gotta have it — like right now," Josh explained. He untwisted the yo-yo string and wound it back up before trying an old trick called sleeper. The yo-yo rested on the ground for a second or two before he pulled it back up into his hand.

"I could be eating a brownie right now." Drake said. rolling his eyes. "If it wasn't for Josh."

"See, I came up with this amazing brownie recipe when I was only nine years old," Josh said proudly.

"He calls them Fudgie Boos," Drake said sarcastically. He was still pacing. Even though the brownies had a totally dorky name, he couldn't wait to eat one, or two, or the whole pan.

"I named them Fudgie Boos," Josh said with an embarrassed grin. He practiced an old yo-yo trick called forward pass. He could still do it! "But c'mon, I was only nine."

"So tonight, he spends like an hour and a half mixing his brownie ingredients in a bowl," Drake said, shaking his head. Josh had

measured the flour and chocolate like the ingredients were gold or something. It took forever.

"And while I was making them tonight, Drake's like standing over me the whole time." Josh threw the yo-yo out in front of him and pulled it back. It hit his hand with a satisfying snap.

"And he wouldn't even let me lick the spoon." Drake said, with a disgusted shake of his head.

Josh practiced his walk-the-dog trick. "And he keeps going 'let me lick the spoon! Let me lick the spoon!'" he mocked. Drake could act like a three-year-old sometimes.

"I just wanted to lick the spoon," Drake said, pushing his bottom lip out in a pout. What was the big deal about a little taste?

Josh grimaced. "I don't want his tongue to touch my spoon!"

"Man! When are they going to be ready?" Drake put his hands on the oven and peered through the glass again. He could see little bubbles forming on the top of the pan and smell the rich chocolaty smell.

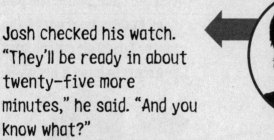

Josh checked his watch. "They'll be ready in about twenty-five more minutes," he said. "And you know what?"

Drake drummed his fingers on the countertop. He couldn't wait anymore. He just couldn't. It was cruel and unfair to make him wait this long for a brownie. "Okay, you know what?"

"They'll be worth the wait," Josh insisted. He wound the yo-yo up for another attempt at walk the dog.

"I am not waiting." Drake insisted. He grabbed an oven mitt and pulled the pan of Fudgie Boos out of the oven. Ready or not. he was going to have a brownie.

"You see," Josh said, practicing more yo-yo tricks. "Drake's going to learn something tonight. He's going to learn that some things are just worth waiting for."

Drake grabbed a spoon and started to eat the unbaked brownies. "Ohhhh." he said. relishing the taste. He took another spoonful. "It's like warm brownie soup."

"He'll realize that patience is a virtue," Josh said with a satisfied nod. He was pleased that his Fudgie Boos could be used to teach Drake an important lesson.

Drake shoveled spoonfuls of warm Fudgie Boo soup into his mouth. Why wait for fully baked brownies when he could have this delicious brownie soup? "Oh my gosh," he said. "Why didn't I do this five minutes ago?"

CHAPTER ONE

Drake sat on the couch in his bedroom totally mesmerized by a news report on the television. He listened as the anchorman threw the piece over to a reporter on the scene:

> I'm live at Mystic Mountain where you can literally feel the excitement, because everyone here is buzzing about this new, big bad rollercoaster called the Demonator.

Drake's eyes popped when he saw the size of the giant ride. It was huge! The biggest, baddest rollercoaster he had ever seen. "Oh my gosh!" he said, gripping his knees. He couldn't wait to ride that baby.

Josh bounced into the room waving a scrapbook with his picture on the front cover. "Drake, check it out!" he said.

"Shhhh." Drake didn't take his eyes off the TV.

Josh was too excited to be put off by the fact that

Drake seemed totally uninterested. "You know how Mindy and I always write little notes to each other in class?"

"Yeah," Drake said. "Don't care."

"She saved every note that I ever wrote her and put them in this scrapbook for me! See?" Josh waved the scrapbook in Drake's face, trying to get his attention.

Drake pushed it aside so it wouldn't block his view of the Demonator. "Yeah, yeah, yeah. Nerds in love. Now shush."

Josh was hurt. He knew Drake didn't exactly love Mindy — let's face it, Drake hated Josh's girlfriend. But he could at least pretend to be happy for his brother, Josh thought. "You know, this is like the nicest present anyone's ever given me. Least you could do is act like you care," he said.

"Dude — this is a news report about the Demonator," Drake said.

Josh freaked out. "The Demonator?" Now he understood. He threw the scrapbook over his head and jumped onto the couch next to Drake. This ride was way more important than any present. "What'd they say? What'd they say?"

."That it's the fastest, the scariest, most intense, most dangerous rollercoaster in the world."

Josh was too overwhelmed to form real words. What came out was a kind of excited garble. He couldn't wait to ride that baby.

"And we are gonna ride it tomorrow," Drake said. "The first day it opens."

Josh couldn't wait. "Hey," he said with a big grin. "You want to practice."

Drake sighed like it was the dorkiest request ever, and then changed his mind. "Okay." He muted the TV. The newscaster had moved on to something unimportant anyway, like a fire or a flood or something. "I'll set the mood." Drake raced over to his keyboard and pressed a button to get a cool background rhythm, then jumped onto the couch next to Josh.

Together, the brothers sat up straight and pretended to pull safety bars down in front of their chests.

"Ready?" Drake asked. "Going up . . ."

The guys leaned back, pretending to ride the giant coaster as it headed up a hill. They both made little chugging noises.

"Welcome, ladies and gentlemen, to Mystic Mountain," Josh said, in a deep voice. "While riding the Demonator, please remember to keep all hands and feet —"

"Going down!" Drake screamed, cutting him off.

"Ahhhhhhh!" Josh screamed, pretending to be on a wild ride.

"Whoaaaaaa!" Drake yelled.

The guys leaned forward, then back, shaking and screaming the whole time. When the imaginary ride turned a corner, they were thrown so far to the left that they almost fell off the couch. They righted themselves just in time to see what was coming next.

"Look out! Corkscrew!" Drake said, pointing and screaming.

"Corkscreeeewww!" Josh yelled.

Together, the brothers made wild corkscrew movements while the speed and pressure of the humongous coaster pulled their cheeks back in a terrified grimace.

They never noticed Megan come into the room. She leaned on the doorframe for a minute, watching her brothers flop around on the couch like a couple of idiots, then strolled into the room with a sarcastic smile.

The guys noticed her and stopped pretending, annoyed that she had ruined their game.

"What is this?" Megan asked. "Some new kind of idiot dance?"

Josh started to get up, and then remembered he was still on the ride. He lifted his imaginary safety bar and stood. "You're just jealous, little girl," he said.

Drake lifted his safety restraint and stood too. "Yeah, because we are going to ride the Demonator."

"The first day it actually opens," Josh said.

"And you're not," Drake said.

Megan eyed the TV. "If tomorrow is the first day it opens, then why are all those people in line getting on right now?" she asked.

Josh didn't have an answer for that. "Heh?"

Drake turned off his keyboard, then grabbed the TV remote to turn the sound back on. They were so caught up in riding their pretend roller coaster that they didn't notice when the story about the real one came back on the news.

Mystic Mountain officials have just announced they'll be opening the Demonator tonight — a special sneak preview for a few very lucky rollercoaster fans.

"You said we were going to ride it the first day it opened," Josh said to Drake, totally disappointed.

Drake turned off the TV in disgust. "Well who knew they'd open it tonight?"

Megan pretended to be sympathetic, but she was loving their disappointment. "Awww, it's okay," she said with a grin. "You guys can ride it tomorrow — the *second* day it's open."

Drake watched her sashay out of the room. He was bummed — big time. He didn't want to ride the Demonator on the second day. He wanted to be one of the first. He had to be. He turned to Josh and got serious. "Don't worry," he said. "We're going to ride the Demonator tonight — count on it."

Josh nodded, just as seriously. He wanted to be one of the first to ride the Demonator just as badly as Drake did. "Awesome," he said, and then he brightened. "Hey, one more quick practice run?"

Drake turned on the keyboard again and hopped on the couch. The brothers pulled down their safety restraints and chugged their way up the hill.

"Okay, ready?" Drake asked.

Josh nodded.

"And . . . no hands!" Drake threw his hands up in the air.

"Wah ha ha!" Josh yelled, raising his arms high. "And . . . no feet!" he added.

Together, the brothers kicked their feet up in the air, screaming. The couch flipped over backwards and they landed on the floor with a thump.

Walter Nichols rushed into the living room dressed in a tuxedo. "Can we please hurry," he said over his shoulder. "I don't want to be late."

"Are you sure we should go out tonight?" Audrey Nichols asked, coming in behind him. She was wearing a beautiful yellow gown for the occasion, but her mind was preoccupied with things at home. Mr. Nichols' grandfather was asleep on the couch. "What if Papa Nichols needs us?"

"Oh, what's he going to need us for?" Mr. Nichols asked, putting his jacket on.

"Well, the man had surgery today, and he's eighty-one years old," she answered.

"Look, he's my grandfather; let me worry about it, okay?" Mr. Nichols asked. They didn't have time for this. Hadn't he already said he didn't want to be late?

Mrs. Nichols was still worried. "Okay, but what if he wakes up?"

"I am not missing the Newsie Awards," Mr. Nichols said firmly. "I could win this year."

"Oh, Walter," Mrs. Nichols said, patting his arm. "You've been nominated for Best Weatherman five years in a row, and they always give it to Bruce Winchill."

"Do not mention Bruce Winchill's name in this house," Walter said through clenched teeth. He was so tired of losing to that guy.

Drake and Josh walked through the living room, headed for the front door.

"Hey, parents," Josh said.

"Bye, parents," Drake said with a wave.

"Whoa, whoa, whoa, whoa," Walter said, stopping them. "Where do you boys think you're going?"

Drake was feeling pretty important. "Uh, to make history," he said.

"We're going to ride the Demonator," Josh explained.

Mrs. Nichols shook her head. "No," she said firmly. "You promised that you'd stay here and watch Papa Nichols."

Drake wasn't going to let something as little as an

old man keep him from the Demonator on opening night. "Fine, c'mon," he waved Josh forward. "He can come with us," Drake headed for the couch and put his hands under Papa Nichols sleeping head. "C'mon Josh. Grab his feet."

Josh followed his brother to the couch. "Why do I always have to grab the feet?" he asked, lifting Papa Nichols' legs into the air.

Mr. Nichols sighed. "Guys, you can't take your great-grandfather to ride the Demonator."

But Papa Nichols wasn't going to stop Josh from riding the Demonator on opening night. "Sure we can."

"Yeah," Drake agreed. "You only have to be . . ." he put his hand about four feet in the air ". . . this tall."

Mr. Nichols shook his head. "The man just had surgery, and he's heavily medicated."

Drake didn't see the problem. "C'mon, he fought in World War II."

Josh nodded in agreement. "The Demonator is nothing for a man who's seen combat."

"Okay, listen to my words," Mrs. Nichols said, getting serious. "You boys are going to stay here and take care of Papa Nichols. Are we clear?" Her facial expression made it very clear — she meant business.

The guys eyed each other, totally bummed. They had no choice but to agree or face being grounded for the rest of their lives.

"Yes," Josh said, kicking the floor.

Drake threw his hands up in the air. "Fine," he snapped.

Megan came into the room carrying a beautiful bouquet of flowers. "Hey, Walter," she said. "Take these to the Newsie Awards for me, would you?"

"Awww, how sweet," her mother said, and then turned to Mr. Nichols. "She got you flowers for your big night."

Confusion crossed Megan's face. Why would she give flowers to her father? "No. They're for Bruce Winchill."

Mr. Nichols' eyes popped. "Winchill? How could you buy flowers for my competition?" he asked, totally outraged.

"Have you seen his hair?" Megan asked.

Audrey Nichols had to agree. "Such great hair," she said.

"It's like cotton candy, but brown," Megan said with a dreamy smile.

Mr. Nichols couldn't believe it. It was his big night, and Megan was totally focused on his competition's hair! "Stop thinking about it!" he yelled.

Megan rolled her eyes and headed back into the kitchen.

"C'mon," Mr. Nichols said to his wife, his shoulders slumping. "Let's just go so I can lose already."

"All right," Mrs. Nichols put her arm through his and they headed for the door.

"And when did she start calling me Walter?" he asked. What happened to Dad? he wondered.

"I don't know," Mrs. Nichols said, picking up her coat. "Boys, the awards will be over by around ten thirty, so we should be home by eleven."

Mr. Nichols noticed a gleam in Drake's eyes. He didn't quite trust the guys to follow orders. "Do not leave this house," he said.

"We won't," Josh agreed.

"We're not going anywhere," Drake said innocently.

"All right. Good night," Mr. Nichols said.

Mr. and Mrs. Nichols closed the front door behind them.

Mr. Nichols wasn't the only one who noticed the gleam in Drake's eye. Josh saw it too, and he was pretty sure he knew what it meant. "We're going to ride the Demonator tonight, aren't we?" Josh asked his brother.

"Oh yeah," Drake said, pulling his cell phone out of his pocket.

"But what about Papa Nichols?" Josh asked. He really didn't want to have to drag a sleeping great-grandfather on the ride with them.

Drake dialed. "I got a plan," he said confidently.

The guys paced the living room, ready to leave. The Demonator was waiting, and they were ready. Finally the doorbell rang.

"Ah good, they're here." Drake ran to answer the door.

Craig and Eric stepped into the living room.

"Hey, Drake," Eric said. "Thanks for inviting us to the party."

"We brought you a bundt cake," Craig said, handing him a plate.

"Uh, thanks," Drake said. A bundt cake? That's what Josh's grammy always brought when she came to the house. No wonder these guys didn't get invited to many parties, Drake thought.

Craig and Eric looked around the living room. It was empty. They expected a Drake Parker party to be full of pretty girls, cool music, and good eats.

"Um, where's the party?" Eric asked, confused.

"Are we early?" Craig asked. He turned to Eric. The last time he was in charge of pre-party prep they had arrived at Charlie Levin's bar mitzvah two hours early. Talk about being over eager — it was embarrassing. "You know I don't like being the first ones at a party."

"Don't start with me," Eric said. He knew Craig was about to start complaining about the bar mitzvah incident again. He didn't want to hear it.

"Guys, guys," Josh said, stepping in to calm them down. "You're not early."

"Yeah," Drake said, leading the guys across the room. "You see this old guy?"

"Yes," Craig said, getting even more confused.

Eric nodded. What was this, some kind of magic trick? He hoped Drake was going to snap his fingers and the old guy would suddenly turn into pretty girls. "I see him."

"This is our great-grandfather, Papa Nichols," Josh explained.

Drake sat on the back of the couch. "Yeah, and he loves to party," he said. "So, you guys hang out with him because Josh and I have things to do."

"You take care," Josh said.

The brothers tried to get to the front door before Craig and Eric could object, but they weren't fast enough.

"Wait a minute!" Eric yelled.

"Yo?" Josh asked, innocently.

"Yeah?" Drake said, even more innocently.

"You duped us!" Eric said.

"Yeah," Drake said, smiling.

Josh smiled too. Maybe Craig and Eric would treat it all as a big joke and let them leave.

"This is an outrage," Craig said.

Eric agreed. "C'mon Craig, we are outta here!"

Craig and Eric started for the door, but Drake had

just the thing to make them change their minds. "Okaaay," he said with a big sigh, casually picking up a boxed set of DVDs. "I guess you guys don't want to watch these digitally re-mastered episodes of *Space Trek.*" He hid the box behind his back, and then pulled it in front of him with a flourish.

Josh gestured toward the box like a model on a TV game show. "In widescreen DVD format," he said with a sly grin.

Eric gasped. His eyes widened in excitement. "Oh my gosh!" He crossed the room and grabbed the box from Drake's hands. "The entire first season!" he said to Craig.

Craig read the back of the box. "With bonus footage!" he squealed.

Eric practically jumped up and down with excitement. "And the alternative ending to episode 21 where Spodnik dies!" he said. He didn't have to think about it. He didn't even have to check with Craig. They'd hang out with the old guy for a chance to watch that. "All right, we'll stay," he said.

"Have fun," Drake said, heading for the front door again.

"See ya," Josh said, following.

"Oh wait." Eric pointed to Papa Nichols. "When's he supposed to wake up?"

Drake shrugged. "Don't worry about it."

"Yeah, he just had surgery. He's on tons of medication," Josh said.

"He'll totally sleep through the night," Drake added.

Craig and Eric looked at Papa Nichols. He looked like he would sleep for the next ten years, let alone the next few hours.

"You ready?" Josh asked his brother.

Drake pumped his fist in the air. "Ready to demonate!" he said.

They turned to the front door again. Just as Drake was reaching for the knob, Megan stepped in front of it with her hands on her hips.

"I can't believe you," she said, narrowing her eyes at them. "Papa Nichols just had surgery and now his own great-grandsons are going to just abandon him? I'm disgusted. And . . . I just might have to tell Mom and Dad."

Drake and Josh exchanged knowing looks. Megan's

outrage had nothing to do with concern for Papa Nichols.

"You want to ride the Demonator with us tonight, don't you?" Drake asked, frowning.

"I'll get my jacket," she said.

CHAPTER THREE

The line for the Demonator was almost as huge as the ride, but Mystic Mountain had done it up right — all kinds of cool, scary Egyptian looking lights, torches, and other decorations surrounded them. Every time the Demonator zoomed overhead, they heard screaming.

Finally, Drake, Josh, and Megan were close enough to see the front of the line. They'd have to step through a giant, fanged, snake's mouth and walk through a creepy tunnel to reach the ride. It was incredible!

Drake counted the people in front of them. "Fifteen! We are only fifteen people away from riding the Demonator," he said.

Josh took a sip of his super-sized lemonade. "I can't believe we get to ride it the first night it opens," he said with a smile. Then his expression changed. "Uh-oh. I just had a bad thought."

"What?" Megan asked. "You might grow old, never get married, and die alone?" She had that thought about Josh all the time.

"No," Josh said. "But thank you for pointing out that possibility."

"What's your bad thought?" Drake asked.

"What if the Demonator's not as great as we think it's going to be?" Josh said.

Drake blocked Megan's ears. "You take that back," he said to Josh. The Demonator was the biggest, baddest roller coaster ever. How could it not be great?

"I'm just saying," Josh said. "What if it's all hype?"

A bunch of riders came through the exit. They all wore T-shirts with a picture of the snake's mouth and the words 'I Rode the Demonator First' on them. They had huge, dazed grins on their faces. A couple of people stumbled like they were still dizzy.

"Oh, man," they heard one guy say. "That ride was insane." The guy gazed into space. His voice was full of wonder. "I feel like a part of me had died, but another part has just been born."

"I don't even care that I puked," said a little kid behind him.

Megan turned to Josh. "Yeah," she said sarcastically. "It's all hype."

Drake watched more people exit the ride. Every

single one of them looked like they had been totally blown away. "Oh man. This is going to be the greatest night of our lives!" he said.

Josh was convinced now too. "True that!" he said, taking a big bite of a pretzel. Then another bad thought crossed his mind. "Uh oh, I have to pee."

"Now?" Megan said, totally irritated.

"Yeah," Drake said. "We're almost at the front. Can't you hold it?"

"Maybe," Josh answered. "But since we're all going to be sitting in the same row . . ."

That was all Drake and Megan needed to hear. "Go pee," they said at the same time.

"I'll be right back," Josh said, running off.

Megan watched him leave, and then checked the front of the line again. "If he doesn't make it back in time, we're still going to go on the ride, right?" she asked.

"If he's mauled by a bear we're still going on the ride," Drake answered. He hadn't waited on line all this time for nothing. Josh or no Josh, he was going to conquer that ride.

* * *

89

Meanwhile, Papa Nichols had started to mumble and groan in his sleep. Eric and Craig stood over him and watched while the old man started to roll his head back and forth.

"Drake said he'd be asleep all night," Craig said with a worried frown.

Papa Nichols sat up. "Where am I?" he asked. "What's happening?"

"He's disoriented," Eric said to Craig.

"What did you call me?" Papa Nichols asked, sounding angry.

"Um, nothing, Sir," Eric said. "I was just, uh . . ." What should he tell the old guy, that his great-grandchildren had bailed on him to ride a roller coaster?

Papa Nichols worriedly swung his head back and forth, taking in the whole living room. "What have you done with the rest of my unit?" he asked.

Craig's forehead wrinkled in confusion. "What does he mean by his unit?" he asked Eric.

"I guess he thinks he's back in World War Two," Eric said.

Papa Nichols jumped to his feet and grabbed a slipper. Eric and Craig took a step back, but the old man didn't throw it at them, he talked into it. "General Patton, Sir!" he shouted. "I've just been captured by two German nerds!"

Craig took another step back. "Uh, no, sir."

"We're not Germans," Eric explained.

"That's just what a German would say!" Papa Nichols shouted.

"Oh, no, no," Eric said, trying to explain. "You just don't understand." He was sure the old man would come to his senses in a minute or two.

But Papa Nichols didn't. "No! No!" he shouted, grabbing Eric by the shoulders. "You'll not capture me! Not ever!" His words were punctuated by a loud thwack when Papa Nichols banged his forehead into Eric's, sending Eric flying.

"Eric!" Craig yelled, stepping forward to help.

Papa Nichols' combat training was stronger than Craig's concern for his friend. He grabbed Craig and threw him over the sofa. "U.S.A.," Papa Nichols chanted over and over. "U.S.A., U.S.A." Then he ran out of the room holding his slipper. He had no idea how long the Germans had kept him prisoner, but he was determined to find his unit.

Eric and Craig sat up with dazed expressions. What the heck had just happened, they wondered? And what were they going to do now?

CHAPTER FOUR

Drake and Megan were almost at the front of the Demonator line. If that fanged head was real, they would have been snake food by now. And Josh still wasn't back from the bathroom.

"Why's it taking Josh so long?" Drake asked, looking around.

"Forty-four ounces of lemonade can only travel so fast," Megan said, shaking her head. She had warned Josh away from the drink, but he had to have it.

Just then, Josh ran up to the line, out of breath. He found the spot where Drake and Megan had been standing when he left and decided to duck under the rope there, and then work his way up to them. But the folks in that part of the line weren't exactly thrilled by his sudden arrival.

"Hey! Hey!" yelled a big, burly guy.

"Excuse me," Josh said, trying to move toward Drake and Megan.

"Hey! This kid with the large head's trying to cut in line," the burly guy yelled.

"What?" Josh said. He didn't have a large head, and he wasn't trying to cut. "No, no, I was," Josh shrank a little under the man's stare. Then tried to explain. "I was already standing —"

The guy cut him off. "No cutting," he yelled, leaning over Josh. He looked like he was about seven-feet tall.

Other people in the line around him started yelling, too. Josh was being pushed out of the line.

"What are you talking about?" Josh asked, getting scared. "Hey! Hands off me!"

"Back of the line, punk!" yelled a lady.

The people around her agreed. The big guy held his arm in front of Josh like a security gate, and wouldn't let Josh move forward.

"Drake! Megan!" Josh yelled, seeing them at the front of the line.

Drake spotted Josh. "Hey. Hey Josh! Come up here!" he yelled.

"Okay! I'm trying," Josh yelled back. Couldn't Drake see that he was surrounded by an angry mob?

Drake didn't want to give up his place on the line, but Josh needed help. "C'mon," he said to Megan, totally annoyed.

"Sorry. Excuse me," Drake said to the people on line as he and Megan made their way back to Josh. Finally, he got there. "It's all right," he said, trying to calm everyone down. "It's okay."

The crowd was getting uglier and Josh was getting scared. He couldn't move. "Drake, c'mon. Please."

Drake grabbed Josh's arm. "Here, Josh. C'mon."

"Hey, thanks man," Josh said. But the people in line were still complaining. "Just let us through," Josh said. "C'mon."

But the burly guy stood between the brothers, and he wouldn't let Josh pass. The people in line egged him on, muttering about cutters.

"No, no, no. It's okay, he's with me," Drake said, trying to explain.

"Now the rest of them are trying to cut in line!" the burly guy yelled, making the crowd even angrier.

"What?" Drake said, outraged. He hadn't spent all that time on line to be called a cutter. He had put in his time, now he was ready to ride the Demonator.

"We are not!" Josh said.

The crowd tried to push both guys off the line, shouting that they were cutters.

"No, no. That's not true!" Drake insisted. "We were right there!" He pointed to the front of the line. The people who had been on line behind him all this time — the people who could vouch for him — were just stepping through the serpent's mouth.

Someone yelled for security.

While Drake, Josh, and Megan tried to reason with the angry crowd, two security guards rushed to the line.

"We've got cutters at the Demonator!" the first one said into his walkie-talkie. "Send backup!"

The second security guard unhooked the rope, and together they pulled Drake, Josh, and Megan off the line.

"Okay, kids," said the first guard. "Back of the line."

Josh couldn't believe it! After all this time he did not want to go to the back of the line. "What?" he asked.

Drake was just as outraged. "Back of the line?"

"We did not cut!" Josh insisted.

"They did too," the burly guy said. "I saw them."

Drake still couldn't believe it. "What? What are you talking —"

He was cut off by the jeers of the crowd. Then three more security guards ran up, and Drake realized he was stuck between an angry crowd and five tough security guards. They had no choice. Drake, Josh, and Megan trudged to the back of the long, long line.

Back at the house, Craig and Eric searched for Papa Nichols. What if he had fallen and hurt himself?

"Papa Nichols?" Eric said, looking out the living room window.

Craig searched in the kitchen. "Papa Nichols?"

"Papa Nichols? World War II is over," Eric said, hoping the old guy would hear him and understand.

"And we're not Germans," Craig added.

"We're honor students," Eric explained.

The guys met in the living room. They had searched all over, and there was no sign of Papa Nichols.

"Why is he hiding from us?" Craig asked.

"Well I guess he's confused on account of all that medication they gave him after his surgery," Eric said.

"Well, where could he be?" Craig said, looking around.

But he didn't look up — that is, not until he heard a scream. As soon as Papa Nichols had the guys together and where he wanted them, he dropped from the ceiling, taking them both down in one smooth movement.

"U.S.A!" Papa Nichols chanted, leaping to his feet. "U.S.A." He kept chanting as he ran from the room, still searching for his unit.

"I can't believe you got us sent to the back of the line," Megan said, narrowing her eyes at Josh when they finally reached the end of the long line.

Drake was just as angry at Josh. "You just had to pee."

"Sor-ry," Josh said. "Yeah, next time I'll just let my bladder explode."

"Thank you," Megan snapped.

"Look, guys, it's not so bad," Josh said, checking his

watch. "We'll still be able to ride the Demonator and be home before Mom and Dad."

"Oh really?" Megan asked sarcastically. She pointed to a sign next to her and read, "Wait time from this point, two hours."

"Two hours?" Drake groaned, staring at this brother.

Just then a humongous guy stepped in line in front of them. He was even bigger than the guy who had gotten them thrown off the line. He could have taken that big, burly guy in a second.

"Hey! No cutting!" Josh yelled.

The man turned to stare down at him.

Josh stepped back, cringing. Maybe the guy wouldn't beat up on a little girl. "She said it!" he said, pointing at Megan.

CHAPTER FIVE

Drake held his thumb and index finger in Josh's face. "This close," he said. "We were this close to riding the Demonator."

Megan stood on her toes and tried to see the front of the line. It was so far away that it wasn't even in sight. "And now we get to wait two hours," she said, rolling her eyes.

"Look, I said I was sorry — over and over," Josh said. "Do you guys just enjoy making me feel bad?"

Drake nodded. "Yup."

"Yes," Megan snapped.

Josh gave up trying to get them to see the truth. It wasn't his fault! But he only said, "All right, then." Josh crossed his arms over his chest and tried to calm down. But then he felt a jab in the back of his leg.

Josh turned to find a little boy and his mom standing behind him. The boy wore a pirate hat and held a plastic sword.

"I'm a pirate! Aargh!" the boy growled, hitting Josh in the leg again.

Josh noticed the boy's mother wasn't paying attention. "Yeah, you're a cute little pirate," Josh said with a laugh. "Aargh right back at you. But, let's not poke other people with your sword, all right?" He gently pushed the boy's sword away from his leg. "Okay?" Josh asked. The boy didn't respond, so Josh turned back to Drake and Megan.

"Aargh!" the little boy said again, poking Josh with is plastic sword. "Walk the plank, matey! Aargh."

Josh turned around again. Asking the kid to stop hadn't helped. It was time to try the woman on line with him. "Excuse me, are you his mother?" he asked politely.

"Yeah?" the woman answered, chomping on a big wad of gum.

"Could you please say something?" Josh asked. He didn't want to have to get tough with the little kid, but someone had to stop him. He couldn't go around poking strangers with his sword.

"Sure," the mother said. "Quit bugging my kid. He's trying to play pirate."

"Aargh!" the boy said, getting in another poke.

"Well, I see where the boy gets his charm," Josh said sarcastically.

The little boy's mother didn't like his comment one bit. "Look, smart mouth," she said.

Josh had had it. First he was falsely accused of cutting in line, then Drake and Megan turned on him, and now this lady was letting her kid beat up on him. It wasn't fair! Josh held up his fists. "You want to tussle?" he asked, waving his fists in the air.

Drake pulled Josh away. "Josh, will you cool it before you start a fight and get us sent to the back of the line again?"

"Oh, yeah," Megan said, rolling her eyes. "I'd hate to be sent all the way back there." She pointed to the end of the line — two people away.

Josh took a couple of steps away from the boy and his nasty mother and then checked his watch. "Man, it's getting late," he said. "Maybe we should just skip the ride and go home."

Drake looked at him like he was crazy. "Oh, you get us kicked to the back of the line and now you just want to go home?" He couldn't believe Josh was giving up so easily. They had time invested in riding this coaster, and Drake wasn't going home without one of those Demonator T-shirts.

"Look," Josh reasoned. "If we don't beat Mom and Dad home they'll find out we left Papa Nichols, and they'll kill us."

Drake refused to even consider Josh's point. "Well, we're going to beat them home and quit worrying about Papa Nichols. Craig and Eric are all over it," he said stubbornly.

Josh stared at the long line in front of them with an anxious expression. He wasn't so sure Drake was right.

Back at the house, Craig and Eric had managed to get up and clear their heads before beginning another search for Papa Nichols.

Eric tiptoed into Drake and Josh's room. Papa Nichols had pulled a blanket right up over his face and was sound asleep on the couch. "Craig," he yelled downstairs. "I found him. He's upstairs."

Craig's shoulders slumped in relief. "Thank goodness," he yelled back to Eric.

Eric crossed to the sofa and used his most soothing

voice. "Papa Nichols? Are you feeling better?" He pulled the blanket down so Papa Nichols could breathe easier, but there was no old man under the quilt. Papa Nichols had put pillows on the couch and covered them up to make it look like someone was sleeping there. So where was he?

Suddenly Papa Nichols appeared behind Eric and threw a laundry bag over his head.

"Hey! Craig, help me!" Eric yelled.

Eric stumbled around, trying to get the bag off his head. But Papa Nichols' grip was too strong. He shoved Eric toward the window and then pushed him right out.

"General Patton!" Papa Nichols said, saluting his slipper. "I just got another one!"

By the time Craig made it upstairs, both Papa Nichols and Eric had disappeared. He crept carefully into Drake and Josh's bedroom. "Eric?" he said, quietly. "Eric?" He noticed the pillows on the couch, and then heard a banging from inside the closet. Had Papa Nichols locked Eric inside?

Craig tiptoed to the door and opened it. Papa

Nichols burst out with a loud yell. Terrified, Craig ran screaming from the room.

Papa Nichols grabbed his slipper and spoke into it like it was a walkie-talkie. "Tell the Marines the beach is secure!" he announced.

The line seemed endless, but Drake, Josh, and Megan were finally close enough to actually count the serpent's fangs.

"Hey, hey, look," Drake said. "We're almost at the front of the line again."

"It's about time," Megan said, flipping her long dark hair over her shoulder. Then she spotted the park's mascot. "Look!" Her voice was full of excitement. "It's Milford Mouse!"

Milford Mouse wore colorful checkerboard pants and a red miner's helmet. He carried a big foam pick-axe and waved it in the air while he high-fived the crowed.

Drake shook his head. "Aren't you a little old to get excited about a guy in a bad mouse costume?"

But there was someone a few years older than Megan who was even more excited. "Milford Mouse!" Josh screamed, jumping up and down and waving his arms. "Over here! I love you sooooo much!"

Milford high-fived a few more people on line, then tousled Josh's hair. Josh beamed with excitement. This was almost as good as the Demonator!

The pirate kid next to Josh missed out on a high-five. "Yo, mouse!" he said. "Mouse," he said again. But Milford Mouse had turned around. The pirate grabbed a hold of Milford's tail and pulled it right off, laughing.

"Hey," Josh said. Poking him was one thing, but this kid had just gone too far. He snatched the tail from him. "You do not yank off Milford Mouse's tail."

"Josh stay out of it," Drake said, imagining another fight.

But Josh was already in it. Milford Mouse felt his tail being pulled off and turned around to see it in Josh's hand. He dropped his pickaxe. "Hey buddy! You do not yank off my tail," Milford said.

"Yeah, I know," Josh nodded and pointed at the pirate. "He's the one that you —"

But it had been a long day, and Milford was mad. He didn't wait for Josh's explanation. "How would you like it if I yanked off your tail? Huh?" He reached around and started poking Josh in the back. "Ya like that?" he asked.

Josh's day had been just as long as Milford's. He poked him back. "Why don't you cool it, buddy?"

"Don't you push me," Milford yelled. "Get over here." He grabbed Josh's arm and yanked him right off the line, throwing him to the ground. "Yeah! Who's so tough now?" Milford asked, kneeling on Josh's back. The crowed egged him on.

"Why, Milford, why?" Josh yelled, trying to throw the mouse off.

Drake ducked under the rope. "Break it up," he said, trying to pull the mouse off his brother.

Milford was pretty tough for a mouse. All three guys were wrestling on the ground now.

The pirate kid who started all the trouble started to yell. "They're hurting Milford Mouse!"

"Security," his mother screamed. "Security!"

Five security guards ran to the fight.

"All right, that's it," said one. "Get off Milford Mouse!"

The mouse knew he'd be in big trouble if he admitted to starting the fight. "Yeah, get him off of me," he said. "That guy attacked me."

Josh couldn't believe that Milford was a big, fat liar. "He started it," he sputtered.

Drake jumped in front of his brother. "That mouse is very aggressive," he said.

The security guards didn't believe them. "Look! You mess with the mouse, you go to the back of the line!" he ordered.

"What?" Drake asked. He couldn't believe it. Not again.

The guard looked at Megan. He thought he recognized her from before. "Are you with these guys?" he asked.

Megan didn't see any reason to go to the end of the line a second time. Not for Drake, and certainly not for Josh. Who knew what he'd do next to get them thrown off the line, maybe even out of the whole park. She was riding the Demonator. "Never seen them before in my life," she said flatly.

The security guard pushed Drake and Josh along. "C'mon," he ordered.

Josh looked over his shoulder. Megan could back them up if she wanted to. "Megan!" he pleaded, but she just turned her head.

Milford Mouse waved them off, and egged on the crowd when they burst into applause.

Things weren't going much better for the troops back at the house. Papa Nichols had wrestled Craig and Eric onto two chairs, and was just finishing tying them up. He walked around them holding a broom like a rifle. "All right, for the last time," Papa Nichols said. "What have you done with Colonel Bradford?"

"We don't know," Craig said.

"We're not Germans," Eric added. He had said this over and over and over again, but Papa Nichols refused to believe him.

"We're from Lawndale," Craig said. He was starting to feel desperate. All he wanted was to kick back and watch *Space Trek*. How had he ended up in a prisoner of war camp?

"Um, actually, I'm from North Lawndale," Eric said. He hated it when people were imprecise. "See, last year, city council —" He was cut off by his cell phone ringing. Maybe it was someone who could talk sense into the old man, but Eric was tied up and couldn't reach his phone.

"What's that noise?" Papa Nichols demanded. "Where's it coming from?"

"My shirt pocket," Eric said. Did this guy not know what a phone was?

Papa Nichols reached into Eric's shirt and grabbed the phone. They didn't have cell phones back in World War II, and the sight of one now didn't exactly bring Papa Nichols back to the 21st century. "What is this?" he asked. "Some kind of weapon? Are you two from the future?"

"Nooo," Eric said slowly. "That's just my cell phone."

It rang again, scaring Papa Nichols. "It's a trick. Incoming!" Papa Nichols yelled and threw the phone against the wall like a grenade. Papa Nichols ducked as it smashed into pieces. Then he ran out of the room. The Germans were secured, but he still had to find his unit.

"Oh no!" Eric said. "He ruined my picture phone. It had all my vacation photos on it!"

"From Niagara Falls?" Craig asked.

His friend nodded.

"Aw, man!" Craig moaned. This night was getting worse and worse.

CHAPTER SEVEN

Josh hit the redial button on his cell phone, then hung up. "Oh man," he said. "This is not good. Eric always answers his cell phone."

"Dude, I'm sure Papa Nichols is still sound asleep," Drake said.

"No, that's not the point, all right?" Josh said, pointing to how far away the front of the line was from where they were standing. "We have to go home. There's no way we can ride the Demonator and be home before Mom and Dad get there."

"Yes we can!" Drake insisted. He hadn't invested this much time in riding that rollercoaster to give up now. No way.

He turned around to see Megan walking toward them. Her hair was totally messed up. She had a far away look in her eyes and a dreamy smile on her face.

"Hello," she said. She blinked like she was just coming back to reality.

Drake noticed her 'I Rode the Demonator First' T-shirt. "You rode the Demonator?"

"She rode the Demonator," Josh said, staring into her eyes.

"Oh, I rode the Demonator," Megan said.

"And?" Drake asked.

"How was it?" Josh said.

Megan stared into space for a minute. How could she describe the ride? "It was like taking a piggyback ride from a wild tiger through the eye of a tornado," she said finally.

That was all Josh needed to hear. "All right," he said to Drake. "We're staying."

"That's my boy," Drake said.

"Hey, give me the car keys," Megan said. "I gotta go lie down."

Josh handed her the keys and watched Megan head toward the car looking totally happy. Then he turned to Drake. "Hey, do you really think we can ride the Demonator and be home before Mom and Dad get back?"

"Okay, let's think this through, all right?"

Josh nodded.

Drake checked his brother's watch. "It's been seventeen minutes since we were at the sign that said two hours from this point. You figure an hour and forty three minutes for the line, six minutes to ride the Demonator, thirteen minutes to find the car, and twenty-two minutes to drive home. That puts us at the front door at exactly 10:58 which is two minutes before Mom and Dad said they'd be home."

Josh's eyes popped. Drake had done all that incredibly fast, and without a pencil or a calculator. "All right, like, if you could figure all that out, why are you failing math?"

"Because this is important," Drake said.

While Drake and Josh were waiting on line, Craig and Eric were trying to free themselves from Papa Nichols' knots.

"Almost," Eric said, working on a particularly tough one. He gave one last tug, and it came loose.

"We're free!" Craig said, pulling the ropes over his head.

Eric jumped to his feet, and the guys cheered as they ran for the front door. All of a sudden, Papa Nichols blocked their path, waving his broom with a wild look in his eyes. He seemed to come out of nowhere — again!

Just as suddenly, the guys' cheers turned to screams as they moved back to their chairs.

"We're sorry. We're sorry," Craig said.

Eric's words tumbled over Craig's as he kept his eyes on the broom. "We're sorry," he stammered.

Papa Nichols tied them up again — this time, his knots were even tighter.

Drake and Josh stumbled off the ride and into their 'I Rode the Demonator First' T-shirts. Their eyes were glazed, their hair practically stood straight up, and their mouths hung open in amazement.

"Please exit the Demonator to your left," said a park worker.

The brothers could barely speak.

"Oh," Drake said.

"My," Josh answered.

"Gosh," they said together. They were totally blown away by the wildest ride of their lives.

"We rode the Demonator," Drake said.

"The greatest rollercoaster in the history of the mankind," Josh added dramatically.

"It's better than love," Drake said.

"It's better than girls," Josh agreed.

That snapped Drake out of his Demonator trance. "Okay, don't get crazy," he said.

Josh checked his watch. Then he snapped out of his trance too. "Oh man! Mom and Dad are going to be home in twenty minutes," he said, starting to panic.

"Okay, let's go," Drake said.

The guys ran off in the direction of the parking lot, but Drake happened to notice that they were running past a group of very pretty girls. He backtracked and flashed them a grin. "Hey, what's up?" he said.

The girls smiled back, ready to ask Drake all about the ride.

Josh couldn't believe that Drake had lost his focus so quickly. Now they had nineteen and a half minutes to get home before Mom and Dad. "C'mon, let's go," he said.

But Drake was lost in a new trance — the pretty girl trance.

Josh ran over, picked up his brother, and ran toward the car.

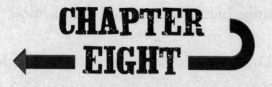

CHAPTER EIGHT

Drake, Josh, and Megan ran through the front door, just in time, huffing and puffing.

"Oh, we made it," Josh said, doubling over to catch his breath.

Drake looked at the clock. "And three minutes before eleven," he said.

Megan was so out of breath she couldn't even speak.

Suddenly all three of them noticed that Craig and Eric were sitting in back-to-back chairs, and they were tied up!

"Why are Craig and Eric tied up?" Josh asked.

"Because your great-grandfather went berserk, that's why," Eric snapped.

"He's an animal," Craig added.

Drake and Josh ran over and untied the guys. "What?" Josh asked. This didn't make any sense. Papa Nichols was sound asleep on the couch. He was only wearing one slipper, but aside from that, he looked exactly the way he did before Josh left for Mystic Mountain.

But Eric was in no mood for explanations. He picked the pieces of his phone and waved them in Drake's face. "And I'll tell you something else!" he yelled. "You guys are going to buy me a new cell phone."

Megan was watching through the front window when she saw headlights in front of the house. "Hey! Mom and Dad are coming up the driveway!" she said.

"You gotta get out of here," he said to Craig and Eric.

"But wait . . ." Craig said. He wanted an apology, and he wanted a guarantee that Eric would get a new cell phone.

"We have things to discuss," Eric said.

"Sure you do," Josh said, pushing them out of the room. "Let's go." Together, he and Drake got the guys out the back door while Megan put the chairs back in place and hid the rope.

Josh and Megan were wearing jackets over their T-shirts, but Drake wasn't.

"Oh dude, your Demonator shirt!" Josh said.

Drake looked down and yelped. That would give them away for sure.

"Go, go, go, go!" Josh yelled.

Drake couldn't think of what else to do. He grabbed one of the window drapes.

Josh shook his head. "All right, that's a choice," he said, wishing Drake had made another one. He helped Drake wrap the drape around him like a toga. "Go, go! C'mon," he said desperately. They had about one second before Mom and Dad stepped through the front door.

"Yeah, okay!" Drake said when he was covered up.

The three kids stood waiting to greet their parents.

"We're home," Mrs. Nichols said, opening the door.

"Hey, guys," Josh said.

"Hey, how'd it go?" Drake asked.

But Mr. and Mrs. Nichols were too busy noticing Drake's new look to answer.

"And you're wearing my drapes, why?" Mrs. Nichols asked.

Why? Drake hadn't thought of a *why*; he was too busy thinking about *what*. "Uhhh, you know," he said, stammering. "I just got a little . . . chilly."

"Yeah," Josh said, nodding and smiling.

Mrs. Nichols clearly didn't buy that explanation. "And so to get warm, you thought it was a good idea to —"

"Dad, did you win the weatherman award?" Josh asked, cutting her off to change the subject.

"No," Mr. Nichols said glumly. "Bruce Winchill won."

"Yay!" Megan said, and then noticed her father's hurt expression. "Awww," she said, and then realized it was time to get out of this conversation. She breezed past them on her way upstairs. "'Night Mom. 'Night Walter."

Mr. Nichols watched her go. "When did she start calling me Walter?" he asked for the second time that night.

"I don't know," Mrs. Nichols replied again, shaking her head. Then she turned to the guys. "So how'd everything go tonight with Papa Nichols?"

Drake looked down at the sleeping man. "Perfect," he said.

"Great," Josh added. "Yeah, he, uh, just slept all night long." That wasn't exactly a lie. He hadn't seen Papa Nichols awake once that night.

"As we watched him," Drake said with a nod.

"Yup," Josh agreed.

"Well, I guess I should wake him up and take him to the guest room," Mr. Nichols said, leaning over the couch. "Papa Nichols? Papa Nichols." Walter shook his grandfather by the shoulder. "It's time to —"

Papa Nichols jumped to his feet and punched Mr. Nichols right in the face, knocking him out. "Ha! Nice try, German," he yelled. Then ran from the room chanting, "U.S.A., U.S.A., U.S.A."

Drake, Josh, and Mrs. Nichols watched him go, totally confused.

Maybe Craig and Eric experienced another version of the Demonator tonight, Josh thought.